Alkyoneus and the Warrior Queen

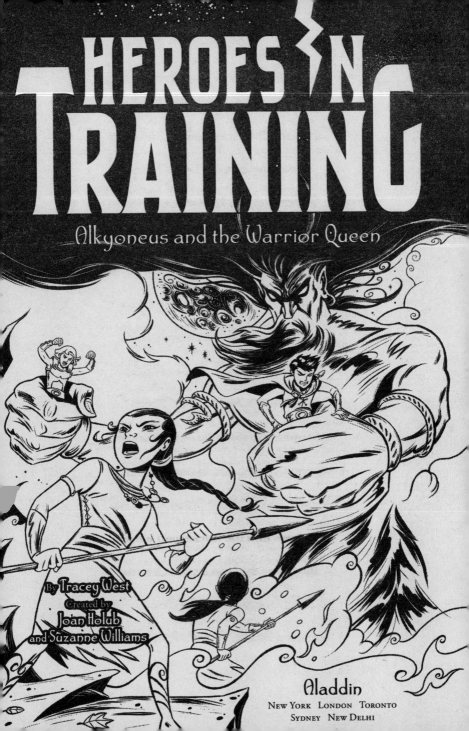

HEROES IN TRAINING

Alkyoneus and the Warrior Queen

By Tracey West

Created by
Joan Holub
and Suzanne Williams

Aladdin
NEW YORK   LONDON   TORONTO
SYDNEY   NEW DELHI

ALADDIN

An imprint of Simon & Schuster Children's Publishing Division

1230 Avenue of the Americas, New York, NY 10020

First Aladdin paperback edition August 2020

Text copyright © 2020 by Joan Holub and Suzanne Williams

Illustrations copyright © 2020 by Craig Phillips

Also available in an Aladdin hardcover edition.

All rights reserved, including the right of reproduction in whole or in part in any form.

ALADDIN and related logo are registered trademarks of Simon & Schuster, Inc.

For information about special discounts for bulk purchases, please contact Simon & Schuster Special Sales at 1-866-506-1949 or business@simonandschuster.com.

The Simon & Schuster Speakers Bureau can bring authors to your live event. For more information or to book an event contact the Simon & Schuster Speakers Bureau at 1-866-248-3049 or visit our website at www.simonspeakers.com.

Series designed by Karin Paprocki

Cover designed by Heather Palisi

Interior designed by Mike Rosamilia

The text of this book was set in Adobe Garamond Pro.

Manufactured in the United States of America 0821 OFF

2 4 6 8 10 9 7 5 3

Library of Congress Control Number 2019952644

ISBN 978-1-5344-3295-6 (hc)

ISBN 978-1-5344-3294-9 (pbk)

ISBN 978-1-5344-3296-3 (eBook)

⚡ Contents ⚡

Alkyoneus and the Warrior Queen

Greetings,
Mortal Readers,

I t's me, Apollo, the Oracle in Training of Delphi. An oracle is someone who can see the future, and I'm learning how to do that. Pythia, the original oracle, is teaching me.

I'm not just a fortune-teller in training. I'm also an Olympian, the god of music! I play the lyre, and I sing, and I rhyme everything! The other Olympians and I defeated Cronus, and now Zeus sits on Mount Olympus, which is a bonus.

As the new king of the gods, Zeus has to solve a lot of problems. Recently a kid named Hercules and a king named Eurystheus came to Zeus with an argument. Zeus asked me to help resolve it. I looked into the mist and saw that Hercules has to perform three tasks for the king, and then all will be forgiven.

Zeus decided to help Hercules, and they completed their first task—getting a scale from a beast called the Hydra. Along the way, though, they made two other Olympians angry: Aphrodite and Poseidon.

After Zeus and Hercules left for their second adventure, I tried to see into the future. I wanted to find out if they were going to make anybody else angry. And I heard this rhyme in my head:

The boy who likes metal will boil
like a kettle!

I think I know what that means, but I'll let you find out for yourselves. Because sometimes it's more fun *not* to know what the future holds!

Catch you later. Don't be a hater! (Still gotta work on my sign-off.)

CHAPTER ONE

Bee Careful

Zeus marched down the path, repeating the rhyme that Apollo had told them.

"Hercules has brought the Hydra's scale, but that is part one of this tale. Now it is time for task number two, and here is what young Herc must do: travel to the Amazon land so green, and get the belt from the warrior queen."

The brown-haired boy lagging behind Zeus

 1

kicked a rock. "You've been repeating that over and over since we left the Temple of Delphi!" Hercules complained. "I must have heard it, like, a million times on the ship over here. I almost jumped overboard."

"I wish you had," Zeus mumbled under his breath, even though he knew it was a mean thing to say.

"Excuse me?" Hercules asked.

"Nothing," Zeus replied. "Listen, I just want to try to remember exactly what Apollo said. I don't want any surprises when we meet the Amazons."

Hercules laughed. "Why are you worried about a bunch of girls? On our last mission we had to face a monster. Getting the belt from the Amazons' queen should be as easy as taking a fig from a baby."

"Girls are just as tough as boys, and they

can be even tougher than monsters," Zeus said, thinking of his sister Hera. "And anyway, the Amazons are different. They're warriors."

Not long ago Zeus had encountered the Amazons on a journey to find the Spear of Fear for his fellow Olympian Ares. The warrior girls had surrounded the Olympians' camp. Zeus remembered them wearing their hair in long braids. Each girl had carried a sharp spear.

"We can handle warriors," Hercules said. "We'll fight them!"

"I don't think we'll have to," Zeus told him. "The Amazons are tough, but they're nice. When we told them we were looking for the Spear of Fear, they gave it to us. We didn't need to fight them."

"Well, I'm ready to battle if we have to!" Hercules said, punching the air. "I'm the mighty Hercules! Nobody can beat me!"

Zeus rolled his eyes and kept walking.

Why did I decide to travel with this kid? he asked himself. *Oh yeah. Because I'm worried he'll mess things up and King Eurystheus will declare war on Mount Olympus!*

"Take that, Amazons!" Hercules cried, and he punched a skinny tree on the path. The tree shook.

Buzzzzzzzzzz! A swarm of angry bees flew out! They started to sting Hercules.

"Ow! Ow! Quit it!" Hercules yelled, and he broke into a run. The bees chased after him.

Zeus tried not to smile. He had a special relationship with bees. After his mother had rescued him from the jaws of his father, King Cronus, she'd brought him to the wilderness. He had been raised by a tree nymph, a goat, and a bee named Melissa. So he knew bee language very well.

"Ow! Ow!" Hercules wailed.

Zeus didn't have to stop the bees at all. Getting stung some more would serve Hercules right for disturbing them. Then his conscience bugged him—in his sister Hera's voice.

Help the poor guy, Boltbrain! This may be funny, but he can't complete his mission if he's full of stingers!

Zeus sighed. *You're no fun, conscience!* he thought. But he knew that the voice in his head was right. This mission was important. If Hercules didn't perform all three tasks, then there would be war. And Zeus didn't want that.

"Buzz, buzz, buzz. Buzz, buzz!" Zeus called out, and the swarm immediately flew back to the hole in the tree. Then Zeus jogged up to Hercules.

"You okay?" he asked.

"Of course," Hercules replied. "Nothing can hurt the mighty Hercules."

But Zeus noticed the angry red welts on the boy's arms. He looked at the plants growing along the path and plucked some leaves. Then he found a flat rock. He placed the leaves on a rock and mashed them up with another rock. He took the mushy leaves and placed them over Hercules's bee stings.

"What are you doing?" Hercules asked, and then his eyes widened. "Hey, that feels better. How'd you know what to do?"

"When you live with bees, you get stung sometimes, even if they like you," Zeus told him.

"When did you live with bees?" Hercules asked him.

"I'll tell you while we're walking," Zeus replied. He grabbed the smooth, oval-shaped stone that he wore around his neck on a cord.

"Chip, are we still going in the right direction?" Zeus asked.

The stone replied, "Es-yip!"

Chip was one of Zeus's magical objects. Chip spoke to Zeus using a language called Chip Latin. To speak it, you moved the first letter of the word to the end of the word, and added "ip."

Zeus and Hercules continued down the path. It led across a meadow and into a forest. It twisted through the trees and then let out into a clearing at the foot of a tall hill. Then the path ended.

"Where to, Chip?" Zeus asked. "Do we climb the hill?"

"Anger-dip! Anger-dip!" Chip cried.

"Danger?" Zeus asked. "What do you—"

Rooooaaaaaaaaaaaar!

A monster charged down the hill toward them. It had the body and sturdy legs of a rhinoceros, and a huge head with a shaggy mane, like a lion. It opened its mouth, and fire streamed out, aimed at the boys!

CHAPTER TWO

Take That, Sparky!

*homp!*

Zeus dove at Hercules and brought them both down onto the ground. The first blast streamed over their heads. Zeus could feel the heat on his hair.

"Hey, what'd you knock me down for?" Hercules complained.

"You're welcome," Zeus said. He jumped up and reached out a hand to Hercules. "Now run!"

The boys raced toward a boulder just as the monster attacked again.

Rooooaaaaaaaaaaar!

This time the fire danced at Zeus's heels. He ducked behind the boulder, and Hercules followed.

"What is that thing?" Hercules asked.

"I need to get a good look at it," Zeus replied. He peered over the boulder. The creature was stomping its feet and swinging its massive head from side to side. Red light shone in its eyes. It seemed to be confused about where the boys had gone.

Then Zeus realized something—the creature was made of metal.

"It's not flesh and blood," he reported to Hercules. "It's made of metal. It reminds me of the creatures Hephaestus used to make."

"Hih-feh-who?" Hercules asked.

"Hih-feh-stus," Zeus pronounced for him. "One of the Olympians. He makes things out of metal. I haven't seen him since we defeated King Cronus. He and Ares, the god of war, went to find a volcano so they could build more things. They must be nearby."

Rooooaaaaaaaaaaar!

The creature seemed to have figured out where the boys were. It stomped toward the boulder.

Zeus reached for his other magical object, Bolt. The thunderbolt-shaped dagger hung from his belt. He grabbed it and held it above his head.

"Bolt, large!" he commanded.

The dagger instantly grew until it was as tall as Zeus. He moved away from the boulder and hurled the sparkling, sizzling thunderbolt at the creature.

Bolt struck the creature's back but didn't

penetrate the metal. Golden sparks shot up as Bolt made contact, and the creature shuddered. Then it shook its head and roared again, this time even louder.

ROOOOOAAAAAAAR!

"You made it stronger," Hercules said.

"I—that shouldn't have happened," Zeus said as Bolt returned to his hand.

"That's okay. I got this," Hercules replied.

He charged out from behind the boulder and grabbed the creature by its metal tail. Then he thrashed the creature from side to side, slamming it against the ground.

"Take that, Sparky!" Hercules yelled cheerfully.

Zeus's mouth dropped open at the display of strength in front of him. Hercules had bragged about being really strong, and Zeus had seen him thrashing in the water with a ten-headed

Hydra on their last adventure. But this was even more impressive.

Bam! Bam! Bam! Hercules bashed the metal monster again and again until it was dented and the red light in its eyes had faded. Finally the monster stopped moving.

Hercules stared at the broken and twisted metal with his hands on his hips.

"Looks like your burning days are over, Sparky," he said.

"What have you done?" yelled a voice.

Two boys were climbing down the hill. The one who had asked the question was dressed all in black, with a silver belt around his tunic and silver buttons along his sleeves. His thick dark hair was slicked back with oil, and his eyes were flecked with gold. He walked with a limp and used a silver cane with a skull-shaped knob on the top.

The boy next to him had brown hair that stuck out all over his head, like spikes. Instead of his eyes being blue or brown or some other common color, they were red.

"Ares!" Zeus ran to the boy with the red eyes and hugged him. Then he nodded to the boy with the cane. "Hey, Hephaestus."

Hephaestus scowled. "You haven't answered me," he said. "What have you done to Leonidas?"

"Oh, you mean Sparky?" Hercules asked. "I pounded him pretty good, right?"

"YOU did this?" Hephaestus asked.

"Well, he *did* try to fry us like a fish stick," Hercules replied.

Hephaestus glared at him and walked to the side of the metal beast. He opened a panel on the creature's back and looked inside.

Ares nodded at Hercules. "Who's the new guy?"

"His name is Hercules," Zeus explained.

"He's on a mission, and I'm going along to make sure he doesn't mess it up."

Ares grinned. "I knew you wouldn't be happy sitting on your fancy throne for too long," he said. "Guess you needed some adventure."

"Yeah, well, living on Mount Olympus isn't very exciting," Zeus admitted. "I just sit around all day, listening to problems. And then Hera tells me I'm doing everything wrong."

"You should come here and live with me and Heff," Ares said. "We're having fun. Even if Heff is in a bad mood most of the time."

Zeus looked around. "Where do you guys live?"

Ares motioned for Zeus to follow. "Come on. I'll show you."

"Excuse me, but I don't want either of these brutes near our operation," Hephaestus said. "It's going to take me weeks to repair Leonidas."

"We won't touch anything, promise," Hercules said. "I could use a break. You know, maybe take a bath. And some food. Do you have any hummus? How about some figs? This bread and cheese we've been eating day after day is weighing me down."

He flexed his arm muscle. "My fans expect a lean, mean Hercules."

"If you were trying to convince me with that argument to let you come, you failed miserably," Hephaestus told him.

"Aw, come on, Heff," Ares urged. "Let's bring them up. I want to show off what we've done."

Hephaestus sighed. "All right, I guess."

They walked to the top of the hill, and now Zeus could see a volcano stretching out before them. A plateau of red rock, dotted with craters, surrounded the volcano's peak.

Hephaestus and Ares led them into an opening at the base of the volcano.

"This is where we built our workshop," Ares explained as they walked through the twisted corridors of the cavern. They passed underground rooms filled with metal scraps and glistening jewels.

"I forge the metal over the lava pools in the volcano's center," Hephaestus explained.

"Ooh, that sounds cool," Hercules said. "Can I see?"

"Only a god can withstand the heat of my forge," Hephaestus replied.

"No problem. I'm half god," Hercules said.

Hephaestus looked at Zeus and raised an eyebrow. "Is he?"

"He *says* he is," Zeus answered with a shrug. "He might be. He's really strong."

"Forget the forge. This is the coolest room," Ares said, and he led them into a cavern with a wide ceiling.

"Whoa!" Zeus exclaimed. The room was filled with half-built metal creatures. One was a long snake with a body as thick as a Titan's arm. One looked like a man with a head stuck to the middle of his chest, instead of on his neck. Another had the front half of a horse and the back half of a rooster. The largest was an enormous metal dragon whose head grazed the top of the cavern.

Zeus stared at them with his mouth open for a second. This was impressive! "They're Creatures of Chaos," he said.

"Aren't they awesome?" Ares asked. "We got the idea to re-create all the monsters the Olympians fought."

Hercules tapped the dragon's leg. "Pretty cool!"

"Don't touch!" Hephaestus snapped. "And these creations are not just 'pretty cool.' They're brilliant!"

"They are," Zeus agreed. "You guys are doing some amazing things here. I wish I could stay and see more of your volcano, but Hercules and I need to find the Amazons."

Ares's red eyes flashed. "The Amazons? Can I come with you?"

Hephaestus frowned. "Why would you want to go see the Amazons?"

Ares tapped the metal spear strapped to his back. "When they gave me the Spear of Fear, they laughed at me. They thought I'd never figure out how to use it. I want to show them they were wrong."

"You should definitely come!" Zeus said eagerly. Having Ares along would make it a lot easier to deal with Hercules.

"You should come too, Heff," Ares said.

"No thank you," Hephaestus said. "I'll be fine here. I've got plenty of projects to keep me busy. Let's go pack up some provisions for you guys."

They left the workshop and made their way down the corridor.

"We don't have any hummus, but there are some dried figs in the storeroom," Hephaestus said. "But I shouldn't be giving you anything, Hercules, since you owe me for destroying Leonidas."

"Yeah. Hercules and I are—" Zeus began, but then he realized something. "Hercules?"

The boy wasn't with them. But then he came racing out of the workshop.

"Run!" he yelled.

CHAPTER THREE

Who's Afraid? Not Ares!

I am not going anywhere unless you tell me—" Hephaestus began, but Zeus grabbed him by the arm. He had known Hercules long enough to learn one thing—where Hercules went, trouble followed.

As the four boys exited the volcano and stepped into the sunshine, a loud *BOOM!* exploded behind them. The whole volcano trembled, and gray smoke spewed from the top.

 22

"Let me guess," Zeus said to Hercules. "You touched something."

"Just a little bit," Hercules admitted. "It's not my fault that the thing caught on fire. And then the fire spread to the other monsters. And then—"

"All my work! Ruined!" Hephaestus cried, running his hand through his hair. He glared at Zeus. "You know, the first time I met you, I lost everything too. You're nothing but trouble, Zeus!"

"Hey, I didn't touch your monsters. *He* did!" Zeus pointed at Hercules.

"Yeah, but you brought him here," Hephaestus argued.

Ares stepped between them. "I can't believe I'm the one saying this, but you two need to chill out and stop fighting," he said. "Heff, if Zeus hadn't found you, you never would have

 23

known you were an Olympian. Or figured out that your cane has magical powers."

"Right. Weird, scary magical powers," Hephaestus grumbled, and Zeus knew why. When they'd been fighting a monster called Medusa, the cane had transformed into a silver sword without warning, and chopped off the monster's head! Hephaestus had been completely freaked out by that.

"Well, that's not the point," Ares argued. "Listen, I'll help you rebuild the monsters as soon as I get back. A lot of them had kinks to work out anyway."

Hephaestus didn't say anything else. He glared at Zeus and then turned and walked back into the volcano. He loudly banged his cane on the ground as he went.

Zeus turned to Hercules and shook his head. "Why do you always have to mess things up?

You act like it's an accident, but sometimes I think you're doing it on purpose."

"Why would I do that?" Hercules asked. He patted his belly. "We never got any food. Do you think Hephaestus would mind if—"

"I think we should leave Hephaestus alone," Ares said. "He can get more fiery than me when he's angry! There's a village a few hours' walk from here. We can get something to eat and camp for the night."

"A few hours?" Hercules wailed.

"Do I need to remind you that this is your fault?" Zeus asked. "Come on. Let's get moving."

Ares knew the way, so they followed his lead. As they walked, he held his spear in his right hand, thrusting and waving it around. He spun around with it and accidentally poked Hercules in the back.

"Watch out!" Hercules cried. "You should be

careful with that—Spear of Fear? Why do they call it that? It's not scary-looking or anything."

Ares pretended to attack the nearest tree with his spear as he answered. "If the person who is using the spear is afraid, the spear becomes a scaredy-spear and won't hit its target," he replied. "It wiggles and wobbles. That happened to me at first. But not anymore. I'm more confident now, and I want to show the Amazons that."

"Well, it would never wobble for *me*," Hercules boasted. "I'm not afraid of anything."

"Except your cousin King Eurystheus," Zeus said.

"*Third* cousin," Hercules corrected him. "And I'm not afraid of him. I'm just trying to keep the peace, you know?"

"Mm-hmm," Zeus said, but he wasn't convinced. As soon as King Eurystheus had become angry with Hercules, the boy had come running to Mount Olympus for help. *That doesn't seem very brave to me,* Zeus thought.

Ares practiced his spear moves all the way to the village. When they arrived, Zeus thought it looked very much like the many places in Greece they had visited. The farmers' huts sat at the end of a big field of crops. Most of the huts had crude wood fences around them, to keep the goats from wandering off.

In the center of the cluster of huts was the village well, and the boys stopped there first to fill up their goatskin bags with water. An old man with white hair and a weathered face approached them.

"What brings you boys here to our village?" he asked.

Hercules puffed up his chest. "We're not boys. We're gods, and we demand some food!"

The man frowned, and Zeus quickly tried

to smooth things over. "Sorry, sir. We're not demanding anything," he said. "And we're not gods—I mean, Ares and I are gods, but Hercules is only a half god. Maybe."

"I *am*!" Hercules protested.

The old man's eyes narrowed. But then he spotted Bolt on Zeus's belt, and his eyes got wide.

"You are Zeus! The mighty ruler of Mount Olympus!" he cried.

"Yes, I guess I am," Zeus said.

The old man grabbed Zeus by the arm. "This is perfect. Come with me!"

"Awesome. We're going to be treated to a feast!" Hercules guessed as he and Ares followed Zeus and the old man.

The man stopped in front of a fence surrounding one of the huts. On the other side of the fence, five curious goats stared at them.

"Hello, ladies. I hope you're doing well," Zeus said. He was always polite to goats.

On the goat side of the fence, a big man with a brown beard was spreading hay. The old man called over to him.

"Nicolas! Come here!"

The bearded man frowned. "What is it, Basil?"

"I have Zeus, the king of the gods, here to solve the argument for us!" Basil replied.

Zeus groaned softly. *I left Mount Olympus so I wouldn't have to solve any more silly problems,* he thought. *This isn't fair!*

"There is no argument," Nicolas said. "There is no way I am paying for the fence. You put it up. It's your fence."

"But I put it up so that your goats wouldn't be able to eat my flowers," Basil replied. "So it's only fair that you pay for it. Don't you think so, Zeus?"

Both men stared at Zeus. He squirmed a little

bit. He wasn't very good at solving these kinds of problems. Usually Hera stepped in to help, but she wasn't here.

"Well, I guess it's not fair if Nicolas's goats ate your flowers," Zeus began slowly.

"Aha! See? The mighty Zeus agrees with me!" the old man cried.

Nicolas pounded his hand into his fist. "Is that so? Because Basil never even asked me before he paid Kristo to build that fence. I could have built it myself, for free."

Zeus nodded. "Well, then, it doesn't seem fair that—"

"Fair? Is it fair that his goats ate my beautiful flowers?" Basil yelled.

Zeus was starting to sweat. He could hear Hera's voice in his head.

Make a decision, Thunderpants! You're the king. They have to listen to you and like it!

Zeus thought about it. If he sided with Nicolas, Basil would be angry. If he sided with Basil, Nicolas might punch him. He took a deep breath.

"I, the mighty Zeus, have decided that—"

"Aaaaaaaaaaaaah!"

Smash! Crack! Crunch! Hercules pounded the fence with his fists and tore it into splinters. The goats took off and ran through the village.

"My fence!" Basil cried.

"My goats!" yelled Nicolas.

"Hercules, what did you do?" Zeus asked.

Hercules shrugged. "You couldn't decide, so I took care of it. No fence, no problem, right?"

But now Basil had grabbed a pitchfork. He and Nicolas marched toward the boys.

"Um, guys, I think we *definitely* have a problem," Ares said.

CHAPTER FOUR

Baaaaaaaaa!

"R un!" Zeus yelled.

"What do we need to run for?" Hercules asked. "I can handle these guys."

Zeus faced him. "I haven't been the king of the gods for that long, but even I know that it's not a good idea for a god to go around beating up mortals. That's what King Cronus did, and everyone hated him."

Basil waved his pitchfork at them. "You kids

better not be going anywhere," Basil said. "You need to fix this fence!"

"Uh, sorry, we're on an important mission," Zeus said. "But, um, maybe you guys could build it together this time. You know, help each other."

"But what about my goats?" Nicolas asked. "They ran away!"

Besides knowing bee language, Zeus knew goat language, too. He put his fingers between his lips and whistled. A few seconds later the sound of hoofs pounding into the dirt filled the air. Nicolas's goats appeared and ran up to Zeus.

"Stick with Nicolas until the new fence gets built," he told them. "And don't eat Basil's flowers!"

Baaaaaaaaaaaa! the goats bleated.

"I don't care how delicious they are," Zeus said. "Just promise me."

Baaaaaaaaaa, the goats replied, with less energy this time.

"Thanks," Nicolas said. "But I still think you should fix our fence. Or at least your fence-pounding friend should."

"Well, *I* think—" Hercules began, but Zeus grabbed him by the arm.

"We'll fix it," Zeus offered. He didn't need Hera there to tell him it was the right thing to do.

He turned to the other boys. "Anybody know how to fix the fence?"

Ares nodded. "When I lived with the Titans, they made me fix everything."

When Ares was a baby, a Titan named Iapetos had kidnapped him. Ares had grown up with two Titan parents and four enormous brothers. And even though they were bigger and stronger than Ares, they'd made him do all the work around the farm.

The boys now quickly got to work. Ares sent Zeus and Hercules to find pieces of wood, and they borrowed a saw from Nicolas. Ares and Zeus did most of the work, while Hercules complained.

"I'm hungry!"

"The sun is shining too hard!"

"This wood is full of splinters!"

They finished in about two hours.

"I think we'd better get out of here," Zeus said. "Before Hercules destroys the rest of the village."

"Now, that's a mean thing to say," Hercules said.

"Yeah, but it's true," Ares agreed.

Hercules looked up at the sky. "It's going to get dark soon."

"Then we need to hurry and make camp," Zeus said.

They walked in silence as the sun set, and found a good spot where they could camp close to a stream. Zeus and Ares gathered firewood while Hercules complained.

"Do we have to camp here? The ground is so hard. And there are bugs everywhere. I hate bugs," he said.

"Trust me, it's a good camping spot," Zeus said. "Before we defeated Cronus, we camped all the time, so we're basically experts. Right, Ares?"

"For sure," Ares agreed. "We camped and we ran. Then we camped and we ran again. Then we camped and we ran some more."

"You sure do like to run from things," Hercules noted. "I think it's way better to stay and fight. Pow! Bam! Crunch!" He slammed his fist into his palm.

"I understand," Ares said. "I like fighting too.

But I learned that sometimes it's good to listen to Zeus. He always kept us safe. And he led us to defeat Cronus and the Titans!"

"I could have done it by myself!" Hercules bragged.

"Oh really?" Zeus asked.

"Yeah, really!" Hercules shot back.

Zeus grabbed Bolt.

"Hey, Zeus, maybe you should simmer down," Ares told him.

Zeus pointed Bolt at the pile of sticks he and Ares had gathered. Sparks shot from the thunderbolt-shaped dagger, setting the kindling on fire.

"That's a pretty cool power, Zeus," Hercules said. "But my super strength is pretty cool too. Did you see me bash that fence back there? Pow! Crash! Crunch!"

"I saw you ruin everything, like you always do!" Zeus snapped.

A hurt look flashed across Hercules's face. Without a word he stomped off into the woods.

Ares shook his head. "Wow, Zeus, you're becoming just as hotheaded as I am, now that you're in charge of everything. And I'm the god of war!"

"He'll be back," Zeus said. "He can't survive out here without us. Once he smells dinner cooking, he'll show up."

Zeus opened up his pack and took out some bread and cheese. He used Bolt to slice some of the bread and then cut up the cheese. He put the cheese between two bread slices and poked a stick through it. Then he stuck it over the fire.

"That looks good," Ares said. "Can I make one?"

"Sure," Zeus replied. "Demeter showed me

how to make this. She calls it Hot Handy Cheese. You take it away from the fire once the cheese melts and the bread gets golden."

Ares fixed himself a Hot Handy Cheese, and a delicious smell wafted across the camp. But Hercules didn't show up. The boys finished eating and washed up in the stream, but there was still no sign of Hercules.

"Do you think we should go look for him?" Ares asked.

Zeus yawned. "He's probably embarrassed, and he'll sneak back into camp when we're asleep. You'll see. He'll be here when we wake up."

Ares shrugged. "Whatever you say."

The two boys made themselves as comfortable as they could with the blankets from their packs. They settled in next to the fire and closed their eyes.

Tired from the journey, Zeus fell asleep

quickly. He slipped into a deep, dreamless sleep—and then something jolted him awake.

It was still dark out. Zeus tried to sit up, but he realized he couldn't move his body. His arms were pinned to his sides.

"Ares! Are you there?" he called out.

"I'm right next to you," Ares replied.

"I can't move," Zeus said.

"Neither can I," Ares answered.

Thump! Thump! Thump! The sound of heavy footsteps registered in Zeus's brain. Zeus turned his head—he could still move his neck—and tried to figure out what was happening. As his eyes adjusted to the darkness, he saw a giant fingernail near his face. He turned as far as he could and saw five huge fingers, clutching him and Ares.

"Ares, I think we're in a giant hand," Zeus said.

"I know," Ares agreed. "That means . . ."

The two boys looked up—into the enormous face of a giant!

"Heeeeeeeeeeelp!" they yelled.

CHAPTER FIVE

Pow! Bam! Crunch!

o my scrawny snacks are screamers, eh?" the giant huffed as he carried them through the woods. "Quiet down!"

"Let us go!" Zeus demanded, trying to make his voice sound tough. "I am Zeus, the ruler of the heavens, and the god of thunder!"

The giant frowned. "Zoos the what now?" he asked. "Alkyoneus is ruled by no one."

Zeus sounded the name in his head.

Al-kee-YO-nee-us. He hadn't heard of a Titan with that name before.

"Alkyoneus is stronger than thunder," the giant continued.

"'Alkyoneus' is your name?" Zeus asked.

"That's me," the giant replied.

"Are you a Titan?" Ares asked.

"Titan, Schmitan," Alkyoneus said. "I don't know any Titans. I only know me, Alkyoneus, and my seven lovely daughters: Sally, Solly, Sully, Smelly, Silly, Steely, and Snarly. And you will make a tasty treat for them when they come home in the morning."

Zeus tried to reach for Bolt, but he couldn't move his hands. He looked down and saw that the giant had wrapped him tightly with rope, pinning his arms to his sides and his legs together. Ares was tied up the same way.

"Zeus, I can't reach my spear," Ares hissed in a whisper.

"And I can't reach Bolt," Zeus whispered back. "I could command Bolt to become thunder, and maybe blast us out of these ropes."

"Or maybe blast us to pieces," Ares shot back. "Maybe we can escape when we get to his giant house, or whatever."

Thump! Thump! Thump!

Zeus's mind raced, hoping to come up with a plan before they reached the giant's home. But seconds later the giant stopped.

"You scrawny snacks wait here while I get the cooking pot ready," he said. "But no screaming! Or I'll squash you."

He opened the door to a cage hanging from a high tree branch. Then he dumped Zeus and Ares inside. Still tied up, they rolled around on the cage floor.

Alkyoneus slammed the cage door shut. Then he stomped away. Zeus rolled over so he could see where the giant was going. Alkyoneus entered a big straw hut that was just a bit taller than he was.

"Hmm," the giant muttered to himself as he walked inside. "What would go good with these scrawny screamers? Some garlic, maybe?"

"We've got to get out of here," Ares said, rolling around on the cage floor.

Zeus tried to sit up. "I know we do," he said. "If we don't find the Amazons and get the belt, King Eurystheus will declare war on Mount Olympus!"

"I was thinking more that I don't want to get eaten," Ares said.

Zeus frowned. "I just need to think. I know that asking Bolt to do a thunder blast is risky, but it might be our only chance."

Ares looked down. "I don't know, Zeus. We're pretty high up here. If we go flying, it won't be an easy landing."

"But we've got to do something," Zeus said.

Then he heard laughing down below. He scooted to the edge of the cage and looked down.

"What are you guys doing up there?" Hercules asked. "Is this some kind of game?"

"It's not a game!" Zeus answered. "And lower your voice. There's a big giant who captured us, and if he hears you—"

"Ooh, I've always wanted to fight a giant!" Hercules said. "Then everyone would call me Hercules the Giant Slayer. That's a cool nickname, right?"

"Please don't fight the giant," Zeus begged. "Climb up the tree and untie us so we can get out of here."

"Why should I help you?" Hercules asked.

"You left camp without me. I came back, and you weren't there, and I followed your trail here."

"We were kidnapped!" Ares called out to him. "Do you think we tied ourselves up like this? The giant did it! Alkyoneus!"

"Oh right, the giant," Hercules said. He turned to the giant's big hut and walked toward the door.

"Hercules, no!" Zeus yelled.

Hercules knocked on the door. "Hey, Giant Guy! Come out here and fight me! And then free my friends."

Zeus and Ares looked at each other and groaned.

Alkyoneus opened the door and stepped out, scratching his head.

"Down here, you overgrown oaf!" Hercules yelled up at him.

The giant looked down. "Another screamer! But this one not so scrawny. Yum!"

He reached down to pick up Hercules. The boy started punching the giant's ankle.

"Pow! Bam! Crunch! Take that!" he yelled.

The giant didn't seem to feel Hercules's punches. He picked up the boy.

"This one looks tasty," Alkyoneus said. "More food to fill the tummies of my seven lovely girls."

Hercules punched the giant's knuckles. "Pow! Bam! Crunch!"

Zeus sighed. "We're doomed."

"Do you think it hurts to be eaten?" Ares asked.

Suddenly a loud cry filled the air.

"Eeeeeeeeeeeyayayayayayayayayayayaya!"

A small army of girls burst out of the forest and charged at Alkyoneus.

"It's the Amazons!" Zeus cried.

CHAPTER SIX

Girls to the Rescue

The girls moved like a well-organized pack, quickly surrounding the giant. Each girl wore her long hair in a braid down her back, and each one held a long, metal-tipped spear. Instead of togas or robes, they wore short dresses made of leather, and leather boots.

Zeus quickly counted them in his head. *There must be thirty of them!* he thought.

"Not you annoying Amazons again!" Alkyoneus

growled. "I can't catch you. I can't snack on you. What good are you?"

Two of the girls hurled their spears at the hand holding Hercules.

"Ow!" the giant yelled.

He opened his hand, and Hercules tumbled to the ground. One of the Amazons helped him up—and then tossed him outside the circle of warriors.

Whoosh! Whoosh! Whoosh! The rest of the Amazons threw their spears at Alkyoneus. Zeus winced, expecting them to pierce the giant. Instead the spears caught on the edges of his toga, and pulled him toward the ground.

"Wha-wha-whoaaaaaaa!" the giant yelled as he fell backward onto the ground.

Boom! The earth shook when he hit. Then the Amazons sprang into action, pushing the spears into the dirt and pinning him down.

"You won't hold me for too long, you wimpy warriors," he said.

"Who are you calling wimpy?" one of the girls asked, and she jabbed the giant in the thigh with her spear.

"Ha! That didn't even hurt!" Alkyoneus said. "You gawky girls will be in big trouble when my daughters come home. They will be here when the sun rises. Sally, Solly, Sully, Smelly, Silly, Steely, and Snarly will make short work of you all!"

Zeus tried to imagine what his seven giant daughters might look like, and shivered.

"Why don't they just finish him already?" Ares wondered out loud. "And when are they going to rescue us? They rescued Hercules."

"And now I'm going to rescue you!" Hercules had shimmied up the tree and was reaching for the door of the cage.

"Just climb out on the branch," Zeus urged.

"It might break," Hercules protested.

"Will you just do it?" Ares asked, his red eyes flashing. "My ear really itches, and I can't scratch it! I can't stand it anymore!"

"Okay," Hercules said reluctantly, and he moved toward the branch. Then he stopped. "Who is that?"

Another Amazon walked out of the woods. She looked older than the others, like a teenager. Even in the darkness, her hair shone with the color of a raven's feathers. Around her waist she wore a leather belt with a gold disc in the center. The golden circle was glowing brightly.

The Amazon girls bowed their heads. "Hippolyta."

"Step back," she told them. She walked up to the giant's head.

"I warned you, Alkyoneus," she said. "You

and your daughters keep hunting the deer on our land. And just last week you tried to snack on two of my warriors."

"They ran too fast," Alkyoneus said sadly.

"I told you to move on, and you wouldn't listen," Hippolyta said. "And now I have no choice."

The gold disc began to glow even brighter. A beam of gold light hit the giant.

"No!" Alkyoneus cried. "I was just hungry!"

The light spread across the giant's body. Zeus had to close his eyes because the light was so bright. When he opened his eyes, the giant was gone!

A bright blue bird with a long, black beak flew up to Hippolyta. She held out her hand, and the bird landed on it, squawking.

"You won't be hungry anymore, Alkyoneus," she said. "Go eat worms!"

She waved her arm, and the bird flew off. The Amazon warriors picked up their spears.

Hercules was staring at Hippolyta. Zeus yelled down to her.

"Hey, thanks for rescuing us!" he called out. "Can you please help us get down from here?"

Hippolyta grinned. She turned to her warriors.

"What should we do with these stinky boys?" she asked.

CHAPTER SEVEN

One, Two,
Three, Four . . .

ho are you calling stinky?" Hercules asked, climbing down from the tree.

"You," Hippolyta replied. "And besides being stinky, you're not very smart, letting Alkyoneus capture you."

"Maybe you could help us?" Zeus called down from the cage. "I'm Zeus, the um, leader of the Olympians. We met some of you before."

One of the warriors, a girl with dark eyes and black hair, stepped forward.

"I remember you," she said.

Zeus searched his mind for her name. "You're Eurybe, right?"

"Right," she answered. "And isn't that Ares with you, the so-called god of war?"

"Not the *so-called*," Ares replied, trying to sit up. "I *am* the god of war. And I have mastered the Spear of Fear you gave me. I can't wait to show you what I can do!"

Eurybe looked at Hippolyta. "Believe it or not, these guys helped take down King Cronus."

Hippolyta nodded. "Then we owe them a debt. Get them down."

Four Amazons scrambled up the tree to free Zeus and Ares. Hercules marched up to Hippolyta.

"You know how you can thank us? You can give me that belt!" he demanded.

Zeus heard this as one of the warriors cut through his ropes with her spear.

"Hercules, quit it!" he yelled. "Let's talk to Hippolyta together."

He jumped up and stretched his arms and legs! It felt great to be free.

"Thanks!" he told the warriors who had helped him, and he climbed down from the tree. Ares followed.

Hercules hadn't listened to Zeus. He was trying to bully Hippolyta into giving him the belt.

"You have to give me the belt," he said. "I'm half god. And if you don't, Zeus, the lord of Mount Olympus, will rain mighty thunder down on the Amazons."

"I will not!" Zeus cried, running up to them. Hippolyta glared at him with her dark eyes.

"Is that why you came here?" she asked. "To attack us?"

"No, I swear," Zeus said. "We just came to get your belt. I mean—"

"Amazons, tie them up!" Hippolyta yelled.

The warrior girls worked quickly to bind the hands of the three boys. Zeus resisted the urge to use Bolt. He knew that would result in an all-out battle between them and the Amazons, and that would be dangerous for everyone.

Better to wait until things calm down, he decided. *I'm sure Hippolyta will understand once we explain everything at the Amazon camp.*

Ares groaned. "But we were just tied up."

"And I never should have set you free," Hippolyta said. "I should have known that no boy can be trusted."

"You can trust us!" Zeus said. "There's a good reason why we need your belt. We—"

"Silence!" Hippolyta cried. "We need to get back to camp, and then I'll figure out what to do with you."

Eurybe poked Zeus in the back with her spear. "Get moving."

They marched through the woods as the sun rose and the morning birds woke up, chirping. Nobody talked, until the warriors erupted into a marching chant. Eurybe would yell out a line, and the girls would repeat it.

> *"Out of earth and fire we grew!*
> *Out of earth and fire we grew!*
> *We're a strong and ready crew.*
> *We're a strong and ready crew.*
> *Call out, one, two!*
> *Call out, one, two!*
> *Call out, three, four!*

Call out, three, four!

Call out, one, two, three, four!"

"Hey, that's pretty cool," Ares remarked. "How come the Olympians never had any chants, Zeus?"

"I guess I never thought of it," Zeus admitted.

Eurybe grinned and began another chant.

"Boys are stinky, weak, and small!

Boys are stinky, weak, and small!

Girls are better than them all!

Girls are better than them all!

Call out, one, two!

Call out, one, two!

Call out, three, four!

Call out, three, four!

Call out, one, two, three, four!"

Ares frowned. "I don't like that one so much."

Hercules leaned in to Zeus. "What's your plan? Are you waiting for the right moment to attack?" he whispered. "Because I've got your back. Just blink twice when you're ready to go, and I'll bust through these ropes and . . . Pow! Bam! Crunch!"

Zeus sighed. "Have you ever heard of diplomacy?" he asked.

Hercules frowned. "What's that?"

"It's something Athena taught me," he said. "It's when you try to solve a problem without violence. By talking. When we get to the camp, we'll try to convince Hippolyta to give us the belt."

"That doesn't sound like fun," Hercules said. "How about you just blast them with Bolt, and then we grab the belt and run?"

Zeus shook his head. "You just don't get it, do you?"

They marched until the sun was high in the sky, and finally they reached the Amazon village. Dozens of huts dotted the green countryside, and dozens more warriors were there, training. Zeus gazed around the camp in wonder.

In one part of the camp was a training course made of ladders and wood barrels. Girls raced through the course, climbing up, down, over, and under the ladders. Over by the forest's edge, Amazons pulled themselves across rope bridges stretching from tree to tree, and across a glittering lake.

Another area held big, round, straw targets, where Amazons practiced throwing their spears. Another target practice featured straw-stuffed human shapes.

"This place is awesome!" Ares cried. "I need to tell Heff about this. We could build a whole warrior training course around the volcano, where you jump over lava and stuff. That would be so cool!"

Eurybe snorted. "What kind of training could you do? You boys are soft."

Ares's eyes flashed. "I train with my Spear of Fear all the time. Let me show you!"

Eurybe looked at Hippolyta, and Zeus could see they were both curious to find out what Ares could do.

"Untie him," Hippolyta said. "One boy with a spear is no threat to us. Let's see what he can do."

The girls untied Ares, and he marched over to the human targets. He whispered to his spear.

"All right, spear, let's show these girls what we can do," he said. He took a deep breath. "Attack!"

He twirled around in a circle, and then let the spear fly.

Whoosh! It zoomed from target to target, slicing through each one! Bits of straw filled the air like snow. Then the spear flew back into Ares's hand.

The warriors clapped, whooped, and cheered. Hippolyta smiled.

"Impressive!" she said. "You are truly worthy of the Spear of Fear."

"And I am worthy of your belt!" Hercules piped up, and Zeus groaned.

Hippolyta spun around. "Again with this outrageous demand! What do you want with my belt?"

Zeus quickly spoke up. "The Oracle of Delphi sent us. Hercules must perform tasks so that King Eurystheus won't go to war with Mount Olympus."

The Amazon leader frowned. "Why would the oracle give you such a task?"

"I don't know," Zeus said. "But the oracle is always right, right?"

Hippolyta looked thoughtful. "I am sorry," she said. "This belt is magical and can only be worn by the leader of the Amazons. I cannot help you. But I will release you so that you can return to the oracle and ask for another task. That is only fair."

She nodded to the warriors guarding Zeus and Hercules, and they untied the ropes binding the boys' wrists.

"Rest if you need to," Hippolyta said, pointing to one of the huts. "And help yourself to water from our well and food from our stores. You look pretty scrawny, you know."

"That's what the giant said," Zeus muttered, and then he yawned. They'd only gotten a few hours of sleep before Alkyoneus had captured them, and he could definitely use a rest. "But thanks."

Hercules turned to Zeus. "What does this mean?" he asked.

"It means we failed," Zeus replied. "We have to go back to the oracle and ask for a new task."

"Can you really do that?" Ares asked. "I mean, isn't it the point that the tasks are supposed to be hard? You can't just ask for a new one. What if the oracle says no?"

Zeus shuddered. "Then I guess there will be a war!"

CHAPTER EIGHT

This Is War!

Hercules paced back and forth across the hut.

"How can we go back without the belt?" he asked. "King Eurystheus won't like that."

"I'm sure he won't," Zeus replied as Ares snored on a cot next to him. "We'll have to convince him. We need to try, at least! Anything to avoid a war."

Hercules shook his head. "He'll never agree. He'll say he has won. And anyway, if we go back without the belt, we fail. And I hate to fail! Everyone will call me Hercules the Loser!"

"I don't think we have a choice," Zeus said. "I am not going to battle with the Amazons over this belt."

"Maybe you're not, but I am!" Hercules replied. Then he stomped out of the hut.

Zeus jumped up. "Hercules, wait!" he yelled.

Zeus chased Hercules as he raced through the Amazon camp, looking for Hippolyta. Busy with their training, the other warriors ignored them.

Hercules saw the largest hut in the camp and slowed down. He walked to the window and peeked inside.

"Look, Zeus," he whispered. "There's the belt."

The belt was on top of a table, and Hippolyta was nowhere in sight.

"This is perfect," Hercules whispered. "I can sneak in and steal the belt, and then we can get out of here."

Zeus hesitated. The plan kind of made sense. If they could sneak out with the belt, they could avoid a war with the Amazons. But . . .

"No," Zeus said. "Once they realize the belt is stolen, they'll find us. They'll track us down."

"I don't care," Hercules said, and he climbed through the window. Zeus watched him trip and tumble onto the floor. "Ow!"

A net dropped down from the ceiling, covering Hercules. That was when Zeus noticed that Hercules had tripped over a very thin thread. As Hercules struggled to get out of the net, ropes attached to the net rung bells that hung from the walls.

 73

"Uh-oh," Zeus said. He started to climb in to help Hercules, but then Hippolyta walked in through the front door. Zeus ducked down below the window.

"Did you really think stealing my belt would be so easy?" she asked. "I set this trap to see if I could trust you boys. And now I know that I can't."

She walked to the table and put on the belt.

"Sorry, boy, or half god, or whatever you are," she said. "What would you like to be? A bird? A dog? Or maybe a rat, like the sneaky thief that you are."

Hercules tore apart the net. "All right! I'll leave! Just don't turn me into anything. I like being me."

"Too late," Hippolyta said, and the golden disc on her belt began to glow.

For a split second Zeus thought about letting

74

her do it. He'd be free of Hercules forever. No more whining! No more bragging! No more destruction. Zeus could complete the missions himself! Why not?

But then Zeus grabbed Bolt. As annoying as Hercules was, he didn't deserve to be turned into a rat.

"Stop, Hippolyta!" Zeus cried, and he jumped in through the window. He pointed Bolt at her. "Stop or I'll fry you!"

The Amazon's eyes narrowed. Then she let out a loud cry.

"Eeeeeeeeeeeyayayayayayayayayayaya!"

The sound of running footsteps thundered as every Amazon in the camp raced toward Hippolyta's cabin. Keeping Bolt trained on Hippolyta, Zeus grabbed Hercules's arm. Then he pulled the boy out of the cabin through the front door past Hippolyta.

There was nowhere to run. The Amazons—a hundred of them at least, Zeus figured—surrounded them.

Eurybe stepped forward. "This is war, Zeus!" she said.

Great, Zeus thought. *I was trying to avoid a war with King Eurystheus, and now I've got one with the Amazons!*

"Bolt, large!" Zeus cried, and the dagger grew to its full size, sparkling and sizzling.

"Pow! Bam! Crunch!" Hercules yelled, and he charged at the nearest group of warriors.

Whoosh! Whoosh! Whoosh! The warriors hurled their spears at the boys. Zeus held Bolt in two hands and spun in a circle, batting away the spears.

Then . . .

"You'd better fear. The Spear of Fear is here!"

Ares was awake! He ran across the camp, and

then hurled the spear. It zipped and zoomed around the camp, and the warriors somersaulted and dodged out of the way.

Three girls circled Zeus, their spears pointed at him. He raised Bolt above his head.

"Bolt, lightning!" he yelled.

Jagged streaks flowed from Bolt and hit the ground all around Zeus. The warriors jumped back, and Zeus ran.

Always running, Zeus thought. *I should just zap them all with a mighty blast of thunder!* But the thought of hurting the Amazons still didn't feel right to Zeus. They were kids, just like him. And it would be better to have them as friends, not as enemies.

This is all Hercules's fault! he thought, and then he looked back to check on his friends. Ares was sparring with Eurybe, spear to spear. Zeus couldn't see Hercules.

Find a high point, Zeus thought, scanning the countryside. *Show them the power of Bolt. Then maybe everyone will stop!*

He spotted a hill overlooking the camp and raced toward it. Suddenly the ground underneath his feet began to shake, and he lost his footing. He righted himself and looked behind him.

Seven giant women as tall as the trees stomped toward the camp. They wore giant leather boots, giant leather pants, and giant leather vests. They had different hairstyles, but they all had the same, giant angry faces, with big noses and angry eyes.

They moved in a line, all at the same time. The one in the middle spoke.

"Beware Sally, Solly, Sully, Smelly, Silly, Steely, and Snarly, you tiny twerps!" she growled. "We are the daughters of Alkyoneus, and we are here for revenge!"

CHAPTER NINE

Revenge of the Seven Sisters

res and Eurybe stopped fighting. The Amazons stopped chasing Zeus. Everyone turned to face the seven sisters.

Hippolyta's voice rang out.

"Circle them!" she commanded. "Then I will take care of them with my belt!"

The Amazons moved to circle the seven giant women, and the giants began stomping.

Boom! Boom! Boom! The ground shook as

the sisters tried to crush the warriors with their feet. The expertly trained Amazons moved too quickly, dodging them.

"Better fear. The Spear of Fear is here!" Ares cried, and he hurled the spear at the lead giant. She batted it away as if it were nothing. It flew toward the next giant, poking her in the arm.

"Ouch! Which of you sneaky shrimps did that?" she cried as the spear flew back to Ares's hand. "You? Come here!"

Ares ran, and the giant chased him.

While they dodged the enormous feet, the Amazon warriors threw their spears at the giants. But they couldn't pierce the strong leather the women were wearing. And the giants plucked out the spears that landed in their arms as if they were splinters.

Zeus thought quickly. He could use Bolt to

stop the seven sisters, but how could he do that without hurting everybody? Then he remembered the hill, and he raced toward it.

When he reached the top of the hill, out of breath, he saw that now the giants were trying to scoop up the Amazons. One of them grabbed Eurybe and dangled the Amazon over her wide-open mouth.

"Smelly needs a scrawny snack!" the giant boomed, but before she could drop Eurybe into her mouth, a cry traveled through the air.

"Let go of her, you big meanie!"

Hercules jumped from a nearby tree branch and landed on Smelly's arm. Startled, the giant let go of Eurybe. She plummeted to the ground, and three of the warriors caught her.

But now the giant had Hercules in her clutches. She grinned.

"Even better. This silly shrimp is much

meatier," Smelly said, and she dropped Hercules into her mouth.

"Nooooo!" Zeus cried.

Then the giant made a face. "Yuck! Stinky! Nasty!" she complained, and then she coughed up Hercules. Three more warriors caught him as he fell—and then quickly dropped him.

"Yuck! He's covered in giant drool!" one of them cried.

Zeus was relieved that Hercules was okay, but angry at the giants. He could feel the emotion bubbling up inside him, filling him, until it spilled out.

"LEAVE MY FRIENDS ALONE!" he thundered.

The sky immediately grew dark. Thunder rolled across the countryside. Bolt flew out of Zeus's hands and shot across the village.

Zap! Zap! Zap! Zap! Zap! Zap! Zap!

Streaks of sizzling energy hit each of the giant sisters. Stunned, they toppled to the ground, and Ares, Hercules, and the Amazons ran out of the way as they fell.

Zeus stayed where he was, ready to attack again, but he didn't have to. Hippolyta stepped forward. The light from her belt shone like a beacon, bathing the giants with a golden glow. From his perch on the hill, Zeus didn't have to shade his eyes. He watched as the sisters transformed into seven brown rabbits and hopped away.

Zeus hurried down the hill, to where the Amazons were gathered in front of Hippolyta. Ares and Hercules stood off to the side, and Zeus joined them.

"I guess we don't have to fight one another anymore, right?" Ares asked the Amazons.

"No," Hippolyta said. "You helped save our village."

She turned to Hercules. "And you—you risked your life to save Eurybe. Why?"

Hercules shrugged. "My mighty muscles were no match for your warriors' spears, so I climbed up a tree to get away," he admitted. "But then I saw that the giant was going to eat Eurybe, and I just—I wanted to help. I didn't really think about it."

"Thanks," Eurybe said.

"Those are the actions of a hero," Hippolyta said. She untied the belt from her waist. "I will give you this belt, Hercules. You have proven yourself worthy. And more than that, you are a friend. We Amazons are strong enough. We don't need magic to defend ourselves."

Hercules grinned and reached for the belt. "Awesome. Thanks!"

Hippolyta held up a hand. "First we need to do something." She nodded to a group of four warriors next to her. They moved to Hercules and hoisted him up. Eurybe followed them and began a chant.

"Hercules is covered in drool! He needs a dunking in the pool!"

Then they raced to the lake and tossed Hercules in.

Hippolyta gave the belt to Zeus.

"Something tells me this will be safer with you," she said.

"Thanks," Zeus replied. "How does the magic work?"

"This belt was crafted by the first Amazons," she replied. "All I have to do is think, and the belt does my bidding. It may not work for King Eurystheus, because he is not an Amazon. But if it does, beware. He could use it against you."

Zeus frowned. He hadn't thought of that. What if they were bringing Eurystheus a powerful weapon? Apollo wouldn't have wanted that to happen, would he?

I hope I'm not going to regret this mission, he worried.

CHAPTER TEN

The Final Task

G ood-bye, Hippolyta. If you ever need our help again, let us know," Zeus called out.

"And if you need our help, we will gladly give it," Hippolyta replied.

The three boys left the Amazon camp and began the long journey back to the volcano where Ares and Hephaestus lived. They reached the volcano by nightfall. A big sign at the base of the volcano read: OLYMPIANS

AND HALF GODS KEEP OUT! (EXCEPT ARES
AND APHRODITE).

Zeus looked at the sign and sighed. *During
our last mission, Poseidon and Aphrodite got mad
at me. And now Hephaestus!*

"I'd invite you guys to stay over, but . . . ,"
Ares said.

"It's okay," Zeus replied. "Hercules and I can
camp."

"Yeah, we don't want to hang out with that
Heffy guy anyway," Hercules said. "He's always
in a bad mood."

"I think he got into a bad mood when you
blew up his stuff," Ares reminded him.

"Nah. He was in a bad mood before that,"
Hercules said. "Bye, dude!"

Zeus gave Ares a hug. "You should come visit
Mount Olympus sometime."

"Maybe," Ares replied. "I want to create a

battle training center here like the Amazons have. Theirs was so cool!"

Zeus nodded. He understood. That did sound cool—a lot cooler than going on another mission with Hercules. Or sitting on a throne and listening to everybody's problems.

"We should head out before we can't see in front of our faces," Zeus said.

He and Hercules walked for another hour and then made a quick camp. Zeus fell asleep quickly, and the next morning Hercules woke him up.

"Let's go, friend," Hercules said, shaking him. "We've got to get back to the oracle before our time is up."

Zeus yawned and stretched. "Okay. But first let's eat some of that fruit the Amazons packed for us."

Hercules opened his pack and took out some

peaches. "Did you hear me call you 'friend'? Because we're friends now, right? I heard you on that hill." He made his voice deeper. "Leave my friends alone!" Then he changed his tone again. "I was included in that. I'm one of your friends."

"Sure," Zeus said. "But you know, you're not one of my *best* friends or anything."

"Well, right now I'm your only friend," Hercules said.

"No you're not," Zeus argued.

"Sure I am," Hercules said. "I'm the only one here, right?"

"Just because you're— Never mind," Zeus said. He took a peach from Hercules, thinking about what had happened since they'd met. "And come to think of it, I'm not sure if I should let you be my friend. When we ran into Aphrodite on our first mission, you made her angry. We made my brother Poseidon angry when we took the scale from the Hydra. And now Hephaestus is mad at me. And that's all because of you."

"Well, maybe they weren't your friends in the first place, if they got mad at you so easily," Hercules replied.

Zeus shook his head. "Forget it. You wouldn't understand. Let's hit the road."

Hercules looked like a sad puppy at these words, and Zeus felt a pang of regret for being so hard on him, but Hercules soon perked up.

"Maybe I'll make some new friends when we get back to the oracle," he said as they walked. "When I tell everyone about how I was a hero and saved the Amazons from the giants, everyone will want to be friends with me."

"Technically, you saved *one* Amazon," Zeus pointed out.

"Hippolyta said I was a hero," Hercules said,

and then he began to chant. "I don't know but I've been told, Hercules is brave and bold! Call out, one, two. Call out, three, four. Call out one, two, three, four!"

Three days later they reached the Temple of Delphi. They climbed up the white marble steps and stepped between the tall columns holding up the temple ceiling.

Inside, a golden-haired boy was strumming a lyre. A bearded man wearing a red tunic and a crown on his head was impatiently tapping his foot.

"You said they'd be here by now," he was saying.

Apollo stopped strumming his lyre and smiled at Zeus and Hercules. "And here they are."

King Eurystheus turned to the two boys. "It's about time. Is that my belt?"

Zeus handed it to him. "Here you go."

The king frowned. "What does it do?"

"You wear it, and then the gold thingie glows and transforms things into other things," Hercules exclaimed.

King Eurystheus tried to tie the belt around his waist. It didn't fit around his belly, so he held it in place. Then he turned to a pitcher of water.

"Transform into a pot of gold!" the king bellowed.

The gold disc didn't glow. Nothing happened at all. He frowned. "Hmph!" he said.

"I think you have to be an Amazon to use it," Zeus said.

"He's a greedy goose," Hercules whispered into Zeus's ear, mimicking the voice of Alkyoneus, and Zeus laughed.

"I don't see what's so funny," King Eurystheus snapped. He looked at Apollo. "The oracle had better send them on a good mission this time. It's my last chance to get something valuable. All I've got now is a slimy scale and a belt that doesn't fit."

"Okay," Apollo said, and he played his lyre. Mist floated up from the floor of the temple.

"Wow. I didn't know you could do that," Zeus remarked.

"I've been practicing," Apollo said proudly. "Now let me concentrate."

He stared into the fog for a few minutes. His blue eyes got wide. Finally he began to sing.

"Good work, you two. You did
*   succeed!*
To finish your tasks, here is
*   what you will need:*
Travel to the world below.
To the land of the dead you
*   both must go.*

Travel through gloom and fire
and fog,
And bring back Cerberus, the
three-headed dog."

Apollo blinked. "How was that?"

"Great job!" Hercules congratulated him. "Really good rhymes."

"Are you kidding?" Zeus asked. "This is terrible news."

"What do you mean?" Hercules asked.

"Hades, the ruler of the Underworld, is my brother," Zeus replied. "He will never give up his dog. He loves Cerberus."

"Then you will just have to take it from him," King Eurystheus said. "Now, that's a prize I like. I will have the hound of Hades guarding my castle. My enemies will quake with fear!"

Zeus looked at Apollo. "Can you pick another task?" he asked.

Apollo shook his head. "That's not how it works."

Zeus groaned. "Do you know what this means? No matter what I do, there's going to be a war!"

Goddess Girls

READ ABOUT ALL
YOUR FAVORITE GODDESSES!

#16 MEDUSA
THE RICH

#17 AMPHITRITE
THE BUBBLY

#18 HESTIA
THE INVISIBLE

#19 ECHO
THE COPYCAT

#20 CALLIOPE
THE MUSE

#21 PALLAS
THE PAL

#22 NYX
THE MYSTERIOUS

#23 MEDEA
THE ENCHANTRESS

EBOOK EDITIONS ALSO AVAILABLE
From Aladdin
simonandschuster.com/kids